Going Camping

by Geoff Patton
illustrated by David Clarke

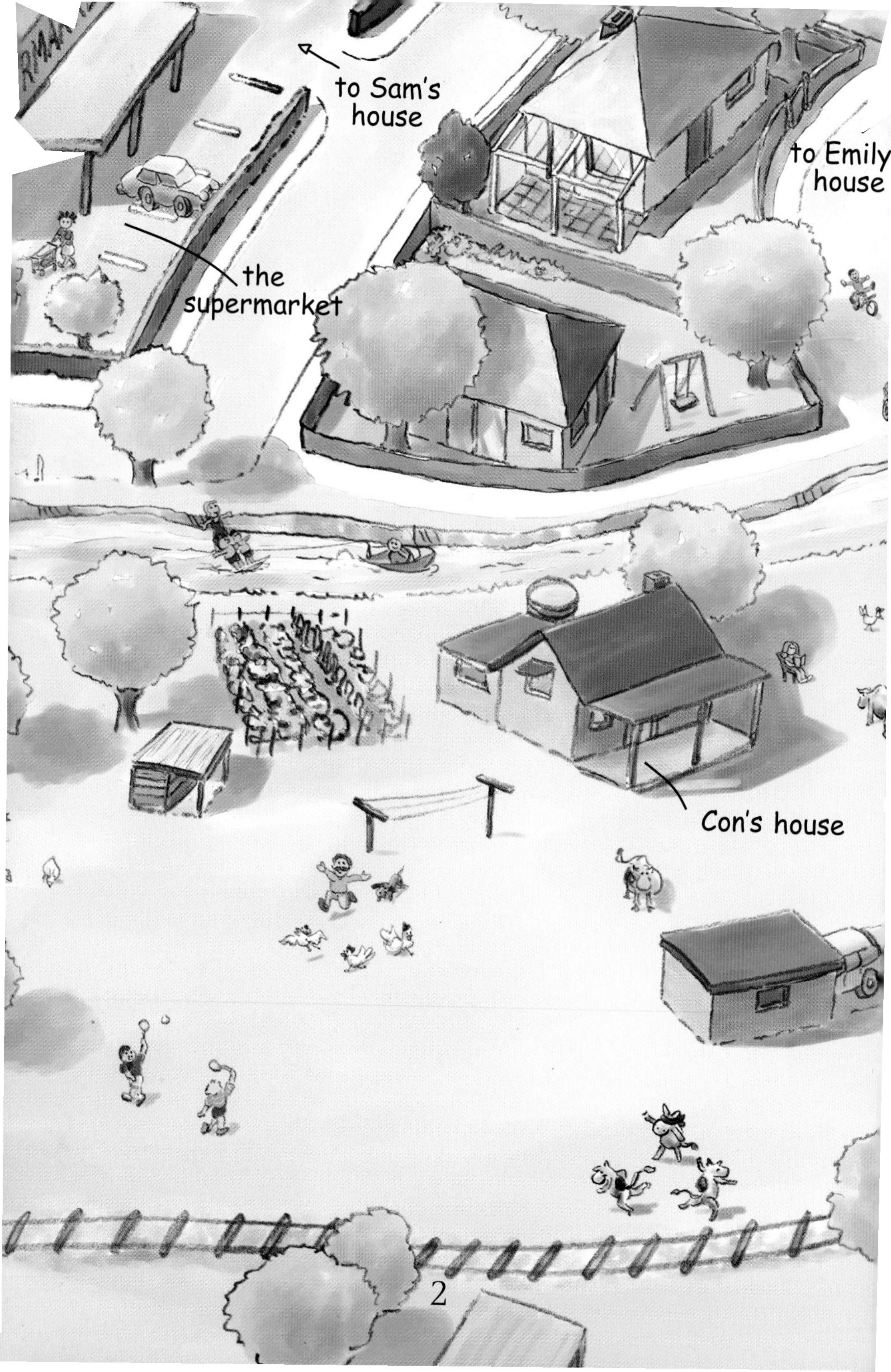
to Sam's house
to Emily house
the supermarket
Con's house

to Lin's
apartment

Hi. My name is Con.

Tonight I am going camping with Sam.

me
(Con)

Chapter 1

Packing Our Clothes

Sam and I pack. We pack our sleeping bags. I pack my pyjamas.

'When you go camping you don't need pyjamas,' says Sam.

I unpack my pyjamas.
'What if girls see us without our pyjamas on?' I say.

‘Real campers always sleep with
their clothes on.’ says Sam.
‘I know that,’ I say.
But I don’t think I did.

Chapter 2

More Packing

We pack food. We pack my tent.
My Superhero Space Tent that is.
We pack more food.

'There really is a lot to pack when you go camping!' I say. We pack even more food.

'Real campers get very hungry,'
says Sam.
'I know that,' I say.
But I don't think I did.

Chapter 3

Still Packing

We pack our torches. Our Superhero Laser Torches that is.

'Real campers always have a torch,' says Sam. 'In case of wild animals,' he says.

I say, 'I don't think there are any wild animals in our back garden, Sam.'

'Real campers are always
ready,' says Sam.
'I know that,' I say.
But I don't think I did.

Chapter 4

Ready at Last

Time to put up the tent. The Superhero Space Tent that is. Dad says he will show us how. Oh no! We say we can do it. We say we have done it before.

Dad says he used to be a Boy Scout. But it is hard to see Dad as a Boy Scout!

Dad hammers in the pegs.
He hammers his thumb. He hammers his fingers. He tells me to hold the peg while he hammers.

I look at his thumb. I look at his fingers. I tell Dad that Sam will do it.
'Sam is a *real* camper,' I say.
But Sam says he is just learning to be a real camper.

Dad hammers in the rest of the pegs.
'*Real* campers always hammer their fingers,' says Dad.
'I know that,' I say.
But I don't think I did.

Chapter 5

No Room in the Tent

The tent is up. We unpack our food. We unpack our clothes. We unpack more food.

We unpack our torches.
Our Superhero Laser Torches that is. We unpack even more food.
We are unpacked!

'There is no room in the tent for us,' I say.
'Sometimes real campers sleep inside,' says Sam.

'I know that,' I say.
And I did.

Survival Tips

Tips for surviving camping

1 Don't pack lots of food, unless you are *really* hungry.

2 Don't pack lots of clothes, unless you are *really* cold.

3 Whatever you do, **DON'T** pack your pyjamas. Everyone knows you sleep in your clothes when you camp.

4 Don't let your dad put up your tent, even if he used to be a Boy Scout.

5 Watch out for wild animals. Even a pet dog can be scary at night.

6 Stay at home. Camping in your bedroom can be great fun.

Riddles and Jokes

Con What are two things that you can't have for breakfast?
Sam I don't know.
Con Lunch and dinner.

Con How many T-shirts can you pack in an empty bag?
Sam One. After that it's not empty. Ha, ha, ha.

Con Sam, Sam, I keep thinking I'm a yo-yo.
Sam How do you feel?
Con A bit up and down.

Sam What would you call Superman if he lost his super powers?
Con Man!

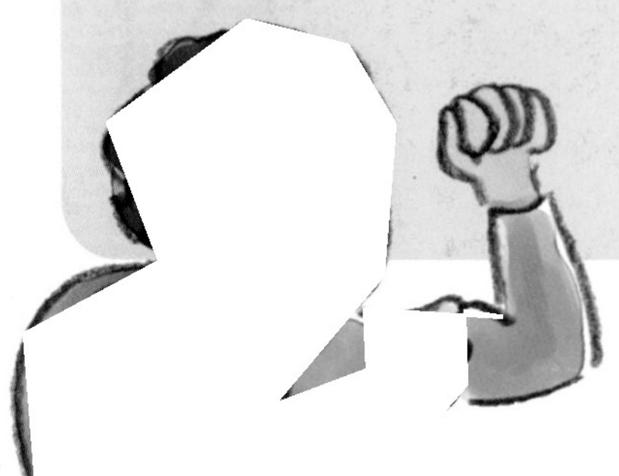